We're Going Camping

A fantasy
adventure story

First published in 2004 by
Franklin Watts
96 Leonard Street
London
EC2A 4XD

Franklin Watts Australia
45–51 Huntley Street
Alexandria
NSW 2015

Text © Dave Hanson 2004
Illustration © Shelagh McNicholas 2004

A CIP catalogue record for this book is available
from the British Library.

ISBN 0 7496 5738 3 (hbk)
ISBN 0 7496 5776 6 (pbk)

Series Editor: Jackie Hamley
Series Advisors: Dr Barrie Wade, Dr Hilary Minns
Design: Peter Scoulding

Printed in Hong Kong / China

We're Going Camping

Written by
Dave Hanson

Illustrated by
Shelagh McNicholas

W
FRANKLIN WATTS
LONDON•SYDNEY

Dave Hanson

"I love climbing up mountains in summer and sliding down them in winter! I hope you enjoy the book!"

Shelagh McNicholas

"I love to go camping... but only when my daughter Molly makes a tent in her bedroom!"

We want to go camping.

But we don't want to
camp in my bedroom.

7

Perhaps we could camp
in the dark, dark jungle.

8

Maybe we could camp
in the hot, hot desert.

11

Perhaps we could camp
in the cold, icy north.

Maybe we could camp
on a desert island.

Perhaps we could
camp on top of
a high, high
mountain.

Maybe we could camp at the bottom of the deep, blue sea.

No! Tonight we'll camp in the garden.

We can go somewhere even
more exciting next time.

Notes for parents and teachers

READING CORNER has been structured to provide maximum support for new readers. The stories may be used by adults for sharing with young children. Primarily, however, the stories are designed for newly independent readers, whether they are reading these books in bed at night, or in the reading corner at school or in the library.

Starting to read alone can be a daunting prospect. **READING CORNER** helps by providing visual support and repeating words and phrases, while making reading enjoyable. These books will develop confidence in the new reader, and encourage a love of reading that will last a lifetime!

If you are reading this book with a child, here are a few tips:

1. Make reading fun! Choose a time to read when you and the child are relaxed and have time to share the story.

2. Encourage children to reread the story, and to retell the story in their own words, using the illustrations to remind them what has happened.

3. Give praise! Remember that small mistakes need not always be corrected.

READING CORNER covers three grades of early reading ability, with three levels at each grade. Each level has a certain number of words per story, indicated by the number of bars on the spine of the book, to allow you to choose the right book for a young reader:

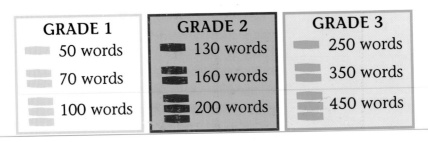

GRADE 1	GRADE 2	GRADE 3
50 words	130 words	250 words
70 words	160 words	350 words
100 words	200 words	450 words